a Cat named Mouse

by Patti Tingen
art by Mary Erikson Washam

Gretta & michael,
Enjoy the
story!
Patti
2018

One sunny Saturday, Mouse the cat spied

a new neighbor.

Mouse was hoping for a best friend.

Springing to the fence,

he offered a paw to the next-door dog.

"Your name is Mouse?

You're a cat named Mouse?"

the hound howled.

Mouse slinked home.

"Why doesn't he like me?

He laughed right at me."

Day after day, the cruel canine teased him.

One early evening,

Mouse tiptoed outside.

A sudden rustling in the grass

startled him.

Paw held high,

Mouse prepared to pounce.

"Stop right there,

I beg you please.

I'm a mouse.

My name is Cheese.

I'm quiet, quick and all the time—

can't help myself,

I speak in rhyme."

"Your name is Cheese?

You're a mouse named Cheese?

My name is Mouse.

I'm a cat named Mouse! And my new

neighbor always makes fun of my name. I don't

know why he's so mean.

Can you help me, Cheese?"

"Of course I'll assist you.

Indeed, I will.

I'll hide in his house

being silent and still.

I'll sneak and I'll snoop;

I'll figure it out.

Little Cheese to the rescue

without a doubt."

"You're my first best friend," Mouse said.

"I'm pleased I didn't eat you."

As darkness fell, Cheese crept next door
to listen and learn.
Soon the owner was calling
the dog for dinner.

Amazed, Cheese hurried home
and hollered for Mouse.

"You won't believe this!

It knocked me flat!

That mean, nasty dog—

his name is CAT!"

Mouse stood speechless. Then...

He planned all night long,

excited for morning to come.

"Someone else will be

crying tears tomorrow!"

At daybreak, the pooch found
the two friends sitting side by side.
"A new pal, I see. How perfect for you
to be buddies with a mouse! HA!"

"Well we have news for you," said Mouse.
"Tell him, Cheese!"

"I think you have a secret;
you're embarrassed by it too.
I watched and I heard—
and right then, I knew."

The dog snarled.
"How could you
know anything?
I've never even
seen you before!"

Mouse couldn't hold it in any longer.
"Cheese hid in your house
and your owner called
and he learned your name.
Your name is Cat!
HA,HA,HA!"

The dog was spinning in circles.

He didn't know where to look.

He wished he could turn himself inside out.

Meanwhile, Mouse couldn't stop his mocking.

"Your name is
Cat!
You're
a dog
named
Cat!"

"Enough!" cried Cheese.

"Now calm down Mouse.

Try to be kind or go back in your house."

Mouse fretted about what to do. Then…

His hurting heart saw the pain in Cat's heart.

Reaching out he presented a paw to the pup.

Tail tucked, Cat raised his paw in return.

And in time – Mouse had his second

best friend.

One sunny Saturday, Mouse, Cat and Cheese spied a new neighbor. The trio of pals padded across the pasture together.

"**Hello!**" Mouse called out.

"What is your name?"

Head hung low, the horse whispered,

"My name is Cow.
I'm a **horse** named **Cow.**"

"That's perfect!" they all shouted.

"Welcome to
the neighborhood!"

The End

Made in the USA
Lexington, KY
06 November 2017